Adaline and Yorky:

Learning to Be Kind

By Julienne Lingle

Illustrated by Sarah Coats

ISBN: 9798353687542
Imprint: Independently published

DEDICATION

This book is dedicated to my Lord and Savior, Jesus Christ, who inspired me to write, and to my husband, my children, my grandchildren, and my friends.

"I won! I won! I'm a better player than you two!" said Alice. "Come on, tell me how good I am! No one can beat me at this game!"

Adaline and Yorky sighed as they listened to Alice brag about winning another game.

Soon after their game, Alice needed to go home.

After Alice left, Yorky asked Adaline, "How can you be friends with her? All she does is brag about herself."

Adaline replied, "Because she doesn't have any friends. Being kind to her is the right thing to do."

"Maybe she doesn't have any friends because all she does is brag," said Yorky. "I get tired of listening to it."

"The Bible tells us to love one another, and God loves her too," said Adaline. "We should be kind to her."

"Well, I'm just glad that she went home," said Yorky, still annoyed by Alice's bragging.

The next day, Mom asked Adaline if she wanted to invite Alice to spend the night on Friday.

Yorky whispered,
"Please no, please no!
Remember, Adaline?
All she does is brag!"

Adaline wanted to be kind to Alice, so she told her mom yes.

When Alice answered the door, Adaline and Yorky realized that she was home alone.

"It's just my mom and me," replied Alice, "and she is at work right now. Mrs. Dixon next door comes to check on me when I'm home alone."

Alice seemed
a little embarrassed.
"I don't get to see my
mom much, because she
works a lot to take care
of us."

Yorky felt bad for Alice and asked her if she would like to spend the night on Friday.

This made Alice so happy.
"Yes, I would like that a lot!"
she replied with a big smile.

As Adaline and Yorky walked home, Yorky said, "I'm sorry for what I said about Alice. That was not kind."

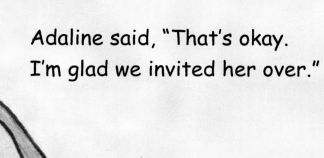
Adaline said, "That's okay.
I'm glad we invited her over."

When Friday night came, Alice kept on winning all the games.

Yorky was starting to get a little annoyed when she came in last. "I feel like a loser," said Yorky.

As Alice jumped up to get some snacks, she said,
"You played really well, Yorky."

Adaline said, "You didn't lose this game. You were just the last one to win. We are all winners when we have fun and encourage one another!"
"You're right, Adaline," replied Yorky.

Yorky felt better after she finally won a game.
"You won, Yorky!" shouted Alice. "I'm so happy for you!"

"I'm glad we are friends," said Alice.
"Me too," replied Adaline.

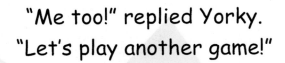

"Me too!" replied Yorky.
"Let's play another game!"

"And be ye kind one to another, tenderhearted, forgiving one another, even as God for Christ's sake hath forgiven you."
Ephesians 4:32

A, B, C: How to get to Heaven when you die

"For **A**ll have sinned, and come short of the glory of God." Romans 3:23 - Romans 5:12

"These things have I written unto you that **B**elieve on the name of the Son of God, that ye may know that ye have eternal life, and that ye may believe on the name of the Son of God." I John 5:13 - I John 3:23

"That if thou shalt **C**onfess with thy mouth the Lord Jesus, and shalt believe in thine heart that God hath raised him from the dead, thou shalt be saved." Romans 10:9 – I John 1:9

Today you can know that you are on your way to Heaven. Below is an example of what you could pray to God to be saved.

Dear God, I know that all have sinned and that I am a sinner. Please forgive me of my sins. I believe that You are the Son of God and that You came to die for my sins. I am confessing with my mouth that You are my Savior and that only through You I can be saved. Today I want to make You my personal Lord and Savior. Thank you, Lord, for saving me from my sins and for giving me a new life in You. Amen!

"For God so loved the world, that he gave his only begotten Son, that whosoever believeth in him should not perish, but have everlasting life." John 3:16

Made in the USA
Monee, IL
26 September 2022

14720061R00021